Holly's Puppies

Rose Impey and Jolyne Knox

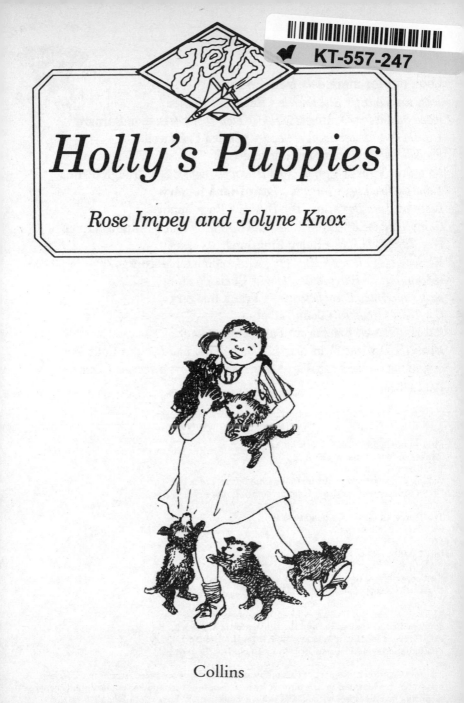

Collins

For Fiona with love

Look out for more *Jets* from Collins

Jessy Runs Away • *Best Friends* • **Rachel Anderson**

Ivana the Inventor • *Ernest the Heroic Lion Tamer* • **Damon Burnard**

Two Hoots • *Almost Goodbye Guzzler* • **Helen Cresswell**

Shadows on the Barn • **Sara Garland**

Nora Bone • *The Mystery of Lydia Dustbin's Diamonds* • **Brough Girling**

Thing on Two Legs • *Thing in a Box* • **Diana Hendry**

Desperate for a Dog • *More Dog Trouble* • **Rose Impey**

Georgie and the Dragon • *Georgie and the Planet Raider* • **Julia Jarman**

Free With Every Pack • **Robin Kingsland**

Mossop's Last Chance • *Mum's the Word* • **Michael Morpurgo**

Hiccup Harry • *Harry Moves House* • **Chris Powling**

Rattle and Hum, Robot Detectives • **Frank Rodgers**

Our Toilet's Haunted • **John Talbot**

Rhyming Russell • *Messages* • **Pat Thomson**

Monty the Dog Who Wears Glasses • *Monty's Ups and Downs* • **Colin West**

Ging Gang Goolie, it's an Alien • *Stone the Crows, it's a Vacuum Cleaner* •
Bob Wilson

First published by A & C Black Ltd in 1998
Published by Collins in 1998
11 10 9 8 7 6 5 4 3
Collins is an imprint of HarperCollins*Publishers* Ltd,
77–85 Fulham Palace Road, Hammersmith, London W6 8JB

The HarperCollins website address is
www.harpercollins.co.uk

ISBN 0 00 675326 4

Text copyright © Rose Impey 1998
Illustrations copyright © Jolyne Knox 1998

The author and the illustrator assert the moral right to
be identified as the author and the illustrator of the work.
A CIP record for this title is available from the British Library.
Printed and bound in Great Britain by Clays Ltd, St Ives plc

The Puppies

The day Holly had her puppies
was the very best day of my life.
It was magic!
They were soft and round
and so cute.
Me and my sister loved them.
We wanted to keep them all.

But our dad said, 'Before you ask
the answer's no. N...O...no.
We are not keeping any of
these puppies.
Certainly not.
Out of the question.
Absolutely...no...no...no...no...NO!'

Me and my sister just smiled.
We'd heard that somewhere before.

Puppy One – Noddy

There were five puppies altogether:
Button, Lady, Nipper,
Noddy and Bruiser.

Dad said we shouldn't really give
them names. He said the people
who came to buy them would want
to choose their own names.

'Well, we can't call them number one and number two,' said my sister. 'No,' said Mum. 'That wouldn't be very nice.'

And we can't call them the grey one or the spotty one, because there's three grey ones and two spotty ones.

We had to call them something, just so we knew which was which.

Anyway Dad had started it off
by calling one of them Bruiser.
Bruiser was the tough one
who kept getting into scrapes
and having to be rescued.
We knew he was Dad's favourite
even though Dad pretended
he wasn't really interested.
He didn't fool us.

Lady was my favourite,
Mum's was Button
and my sister had *two* favourites:
Nipper and Noddy.

We couldn't bear to think of any
of the puppies going to new homes.
But we didn't mind too much
with the first one, because she was
going to Grandma and Grandad's.
So we knew we'd still see her.

Grandma and Grandad were
used to having a dog.

They had one
called Tess,
when Mum
was little.

Then one
called Bunty,

and then one
called Heidi.

Heidi died before we were born
and Grandma and Grandad were
too upset to get another one.
Until now.

I wanted them to choose Lady.
My sister wanted them to choose
Nipper or Noddy. We started arguing.
Mum said,

Now stop that.
We must let Grandma
and Grandad choose
the one they want.
We can't choose
for them.

When the puppies were a month old
Grandma and Grandad came to stay.

All weekend they talked about
what kind of puppy they wanted.

'You can't tell how big they'll grow,'
said Grandad. 'Holly's not very
big, but we don't know who the
father was.'

We hadn't thought about that.
He could have been any shape or size.
Every time we saw a dog in the street
or in our local park we wondered
if he was the one.

'You can't tell that yet, either,' said
Grandad, 'until they're older and
get their bark.'

'Well, we don't want one that's too lively,' said Grandma. 'We don't want to be racing around at our age.' Grandad picked up Noddy.

Right. Then I think this is the one.

We'd called her Noddy, because she was always nodding off. She was the first one to settle down for a sleep and the last to wake up.

Even when Bruiser climbed over her,
Noddy still nodded off.

She was very sweet,
but she was a bit too sleepy for me.
That's why she was just right for
Grandma and Grandad.
When they had their afternoon nap,
Noddy had one with them.

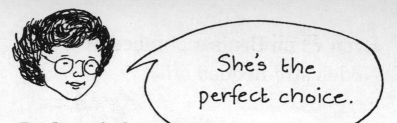

She's the perfect choice.

Dad smiled too.
'One down and four
to go,' he said,
under his breath.
But we'd heard him.

We gave him one
of our looks.

It's no good looking
like that. I've told you, they've all
got to go. You can't keep any of
them. Don't even think about it.

But me and my sister kept
our fingers tightly crossed.
Perhaps no one would
want the others.
Then we'd have
to keep them.

16

Puppy Two – Lady

When the puppies were five weeks old Dad put a card in the paper shop window. He wrote:

Four puppies for
Sale
Ring:
Paul Buckley
2794670

Lots of people came round to see the puppies.

On Monday a posh lady called
Mrs Pilkington-Potts came round.

She was looking
for a puppy to
take the place of
her little Trinket.
Trinket had died
six months ago.

When she showed
us her photo,
she started to
get upset.

She went away
without buying
a puppy.
Mum said, 'I
don't think she's
ready for another
dog just yet.'

On Tuesday, Camilla Carr,
a horrible girl from my school
came round.
She's really spoiled.
Her parents give her
everything she wants.
When she stroked Nipper
he nipped her finger
and she started to cry.

I don't want a puppy any more. Not if it bites.

I didn't say a word,
but, afterwards,
Mum told me off
for grinning.

On Wednesday a lady came
with her two little boys.
They were a pair of pests.
While the lady
had a cup of tea
they kept fighting,

and pulling
the puppies' tails.
As she left, she said,

I'll talk to my husband
about it. Perhaps
we'll get them
one each.

But, when she'd gone,
my sister said,

They're not having
any of our puppies.
Certainly not.
Out of the question.
Absolutely no...
no... no... no...
NO!

You could tell she meant it.
Mum and Dad burst out laughing.

On Thursday Mrs Baker came
to look at the puppies.
She's our lollipop lady
from school. She didn't
buy one either.
She said it had to be
a really little dog.
But we couldn't
be sure.

Holly could have
mated with an Alsation.

'Or a Doberman,' I said.
'Or a Great Dane,' said my sister.
'Or an elephant,' said Dad.

That made us giggle.

Mum shook her head.
'Sometimes,' she said, 'it's like
having three children in this family.'

On Friday, when the evening paper arrived, we went out to talk to Ruby, the paper girl. She's our friend. We invited her in to see the puppies.

Lady was her favourite too,
because she was so pretty.
Lady had the biggest eyes
and the softest fur.

She liked sitting on
my knee while I
stroked her.

Or on the arm of Dad's chair.

Just look at her. She's like the Queen of Sheba.

Ruby's mum and dad said she could have Lady as a birthday present.

It's not fair, Lady was my favourite.

But Mum said, 'Ruby only lives round the corner. You can go and see her whenever you like.'

Two down;
three to go.

But this time Dad didn't grin.
He could see I was upset.

'We've still got three puppies left,'
said my sister.

Puppy Three – Nipper

When the puppies were six weeks old, they really began to find their way around.

If one set off on an expedition,

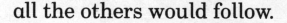

all the others would follow.

Five fat little bottoms would disappear

down the garden

or up the stairs

or into the shoe cupboard
– if anyone left the door open.

They liked climbing.
Mostly they liked climbing people.
When me and my sister were
lying on the floor watching TV
the puppies climbed up
and lay on top of us.

When Mum called us for tea,
they'd hitch a ride.
One time my sister had all five
puppies hanging from her.

Now that Noddy was going to live
with Grandma and Grandad,
Nipper was my sister's real favourite.
We called him that for obvious
reasons.

He was always
nipping us.
But we didn't mind.
It didn't really hurt.

My sister knew she couldn't keep
him, but she couldn't bear to lose
him either.

So she started
to make plans.
She didn't tell
Mum and Dad.
She didn't even
tell me.

The first we knew about it was one night when her teacher from school rang.

Oh, boy, my sister was in big trouble! I'll tell you what she'd done.

She'd been trying to persuade her friends at school to have Nipper. She'd been using her pocket money to buy sweets to help persuade them.

Some of their parents had found out and rung school to complain.

It's called bribery. It's against the law you know.

You could get arrested.

Don't be silly. Don't go upsetting her.

My sister burst into tears. Mum sat her on her knee.

'Now, come on. You're all right.
You must understand, though,
that what you did was wrong.'

'But Gina wants a puppy,'
said my sister.

Gina's my sister's best friend. 'Gina
can't just decide to have a puppy,'
said Mum. 'She has to get her
parents' permission. Just like you
did.'

And Gina's mum and
dad have probably got
more sense than yours.

But Dad was wrong.
Every day Gina begged them
to let her have a puppy.

She did all the things we'd done
to try to persuade them.
And she didn't give up until they said,
'Okay, okay, we give in.
You can have one.'
Then she cheered up.
And so did my sister.
They were over the moon.

OVER THE MOON

Dad was quite pleased too.
'That's three puppies gone,' he said.
'Only two left.'
Only two puppies, we couldn't bear it.

Puppy Four – Button

The puppies were seven weeks old.
They hadn't gone to their new
homes yet because the vet said they
should stay with their mum until
they were at least six weeks old.

So they could
go now.

'Well, she said six or eight weeks,'
Mum reminded him.

A little longer
won't hurt.

Me and my sister agreed with Mum.
We were on her side.

Mum's favourite was Button.
She'd chosen that name because
she said he was as bright as a button.

'He was just exploring,' said Mum.
'That's a sign of intelligence.
You mark my words,
this one's the cleverest.'

Dad didn't agree with Mum,
but Mr Moore did.
Mr Moore was the teacher at the
Dog Training Class that Holly
went to.

He called round to see Holly's
puppies. Dad told him there were
two puppies who still needed a home.
But he didn't say which two.

Mr Moore watched the puppies play.
Then he picked each of them up.
'They're five grand little puppies,'
he said, scooping up Button.

But this is the best of the bunch. This is the one I'd like.

We were really
surprised. We didn't
know he wanted
one. The puppy was
for his grandson.

I'll want to train him
first and this one's the
cleverest. You can tell
at a glance. He's as
bright as a button.

What did
I tell you?

Mum grinned at Dad.
Dad rolled his eyes.

Yes, yes.
You're right.
As usual.

Now, all the puppies had got a home,
except one.
Guess whose favourite he was.

'It's not fair,' said my sister.
'It's not my fault no one wants him,'
said Dad. 'You're a menace,
you are,' he told Bruiser.

'He's not a menace,' said Mum.
'He just needs . . .'

I know. He just
needs training.
Well, someone else
can have that job.
I'll be glad to
see the back
of him.

And he put the toe of his shoe
under Bruiser's bottom.

Bruiser did a somersault.
He didn't know what had
happened to him.

'Oh, Dad!' we said. 'Don't do that.'
'That wasn't very nice,' said Mum.

But Dad laughed
and laughed.
Sometimes he thinks
he's so funny.

But Bruiser got his own back.

Later that day he did a little puddle
. . . in Dad's slipper!

Dad didn't think
that was funny,
but the rest
of us did.

We laughed
and laughed.

It serves you right.

'Oh, thanks,' said Dad. 'You wait,'
he told Bruiser.

You'll be next to go.

Now there was only one puppy who
hadn't got a home.
We couldn't bear it.

Puppy Five – Bruiser

A week later the puppies were ready
to go to their new homes.
Grandma and Grandad came
to pick up Noddy.

When we waved them off in the car,
my sister started to cry.

Grandma waved
Noddy's paw.

That made me
want to cry too.

Mr Moore came the next day
to collect Button.
He brought his grandson with him.

You could tell he really loved
the puppy, so it wasn't so bad.
We knew he'd got a good home.

The same day Ruby took Lady home. I walked round with her.

Then I walked home all on my own. I had a little cry.

The next day, when Gina's mum and dad came to collect Nipper, they took my sister back with them to stay for the weekend.

I played with Bruiser that night because we both felt lonely.

Dad was still trying to find a home
for Bruiser. A few more people came
to see him.

Holly must have known they were
coming to take her last puppy away,
because she growled at everyone.

No one seemed to want Bruiser.

We didn't mind.
And Bruiser didn't mind.
But Dad minded.

We've got one dog already, we're not having two.

Then Bruiser did something bad.
In fact it was terrible.
Bruiser was always chewing things,
like Holly did when we first had her.
One day, while we were having tea,
he tried to eat one of Dad's
Beatles tapes.

Oh no!

My sister found him with a long piece
of it hanging out of his mouth.
'Don't pull it, whatever you do,'
shouted Mum. 'He might choke.
We'll have to get him to the vet's.'

Be careful!

The tape was all caught up
in his stomach.
The vet said Bruiser might die,
unless he had an operation.
We had to leave him at the vet's.
It was terrible.

That night me and my sister
didn't want to go to bed.
Mum gave us a cuddle and
tried to cheer us up.
But she couldn't cheer Dad up.

He was so miserable.
He said it was
all his fault.

I shouldn't have left the tape where he could get it.

He said he would really miss Bruiser
if anything happened to him.
Then he said the best thing of all.

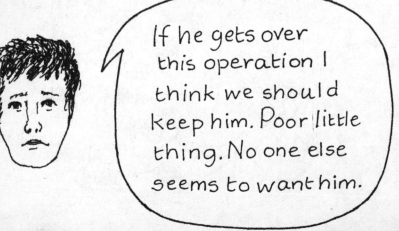

If he gets over this operation I think we should keep him. Poor little thing. No one else seems to want him.

'Yippee!' said my sister.
We both ran over and gave
Dad a big, big hug.

Bruiser did get better.
In fact you'd never have guessed
he'd had an accident.
He was soon back to his tricks.

Holly was pleased to see him
and so was Dad.
'I always knew you had a
soft spot for that one,' said Mum.

'What shall we call him?' said
my sister.
'What do you mean?' said Dad.
'Well,' said Mum, 'Bruiser's not
a very nice name, is it?'

My sister ran to find the book of
dogs' names.

We could
have a vote.

'Oh, no,' said Dad. 'Bruiser's a
perfectly good name. We're not
starting that again.'

Me and my sister nodded
and smiled. 'Okay,' we said.
'You're the boss.'